BUDDY THE FILES

The Case of the
P-O-U-N-D
Pet

Dori Hillestad Butler
PICTURES BY DANA SULLIVAN

For all the kids who asked,
"Can you write more Buddy Files books?"

POINT VISTA PRESS

Published in 2018
Kirkland, Washington

Book design by Kathryn Campbell

Library of Congress Cataloging-in-Publication Data

Names: Butler, Dori Hillestad, author | Sullivan, Dana, illustrator.
Title: The Buddy files : the case of the P-O-U-N-D pet / Dori Hillestad Butler ;
pictures by Dana Sullivan.
Description: Kirkland, WA: Point Vista Press, 2018.
Identifiers: ISBN 978-1-946942-00-5 (pbk.)
978-1-946942-01-2 (Hardcover) | 978-1-946942-02-9 (Kindle)
Summary: When Buddy the dog is accused of stealing a beloved stuffed toy,
he must solve the mystery to clear his good name.
Subjects: LCSH Dogs—Juvenile fiction. | Mystery and detective stories.
| BISAC JUVENILE FICTION / General.
Classifications: LCC PZ7.B9759 Bu 2018 | [E]—dc23

LC record available at http://lccn.loc.gov/2017938931

Manufactured in the United States of America

TABLE OF CONTENTS

1

New Neighbors

Hello!

My name is Buddy. I'm a detective.

I'm also a therapy dog. I live with Connor and Mom. They are my people. They take me to school every day so I can help kids. Sometimes I listen to kids read. Sometimes I listen to their problems. Sometimes I just let them pet me. That's what being a therapy dog is all about.

I haven't always been a therapy dog. And I haven't always lived with Connor and Mom.

I used to live with Kayla and another mom and dad. They were my people before Connor and Mom were my people. Kayla and her family moved away eleventy-three months ago. Kayla's uncle was supposed to take care of me, but he took me to the **P-O-U-N-D**.

When Connor and Mom came to the **P-O-U-N-D** I decided to adopt them. Good thing I did, because guess what? They moved into the house behind my old house. That means I can keep an eye on my old house.

For a long time, no one lived there. Then four or nine days ago a girl named Adara moved in. I like Adara. She smells like apples and paint.

Unfortunately, Adara does not like me. I think she's scared of me, but I don't know why. I'm not scary.

My friend Mouse knows how I feel. Mouse is a dog, not a mouse. Some humans are scared of him because he's BIG. They don't know he wouldn't hurt a flea.

"Mouse? Hey, Mouse!" I call. Mouse is an outdoor dog, so I can talk to him whenever I'm outside.

"HI, BUDDY!" Mouse calls back. "WHAT'S ON YOUR MIND?" Mouse is the biggest, LOUDEST dog on our street.

"The new girl, Adara. She's on my mind," I tell Mouse. "She doesn't like me. What can I do to make her like me?"

"YOU CAN'T *MAKE* A HUMAN LIKE YOU, BUDDY," Mouse says.

"Why not?" I ask.

"YOU JUST CAN'T," Mouse says. "SOME HUMANS DON'T LIKE DOGS. THERE'S NOTHING YOU CAN DO ABOUT IT."

"But that's not fair," I say.

"I KNOW," Mouse says. "BUT THAT'S THE WAY IT IS."

I think Mouse is wrong. I'm going to show Adara what a good dog I am. Then she'll like me. I know she will.

Nine or five days later I am walking to school with Connor and Michael. Michael is one of Mouse's humans.

Adara is walking to school, too. She's walking in front of us with some first-graders named Jemma and Caroline. I know them because they read to me at school.

All those girls are carrying stuffed animals. Adara's stuffed animal is a DOG!

A fuzzy dog with floppy ears. If she likes stuffed dogs, she should like real dogs, too, don't you think?

Adara keeps glancing at me over her shoulder.

"Hi, Adara!" I smile and wag my tail.

She does not smile back. She hugs her dog tight to her chest and keeps right on walking.

I grab a stick from the grass and show it to her. "Wanna play Fetch?" I ask. Most humans LOVE to play Fetch.

Connor pulls me back. "Slow down, Buddy. And drop the stick. We're not playing Fetch. We're walking to school."

"Can't we do both?" I ask. If I play Fetch with Adara, then maybe she'll like me.

Connor stops walking. "Drop it," he says again.

"Fine." I drop the stick.

We start walking again. Connor and Michael talk about boring human stuff. I wait for Adara to turn around so I can smile at her again.

Suddenly, a boy around Adara's size runs up behind us. He yanks the stuffed dog from Adara's hands and zooms away with it.

Erik!" Adara cries, hurrying after him. "Stop! That's *my* Rufus! Bring him back!"

Erik doesn't stop. He's running and laughing like they're playing a fun game. But I can tell Adara isn't having fun.

"I'll get your Rufus," I tell her. CHARGE! I pull my leash out of Connor's hands and chase Erik down the street.

"Buddy, no!" Connor yells.

"I'm going to get Rufus," I tell Connor. "I'll be back."

My paws pound against the pavement. I chase Erik onto the grass and knock him down. Rufus flies from Erik's hands and I grab him with my teeth.

Yuck! I spit him right back out. Rufus

has glitter on his shirt. I don't like glitter. It gets stuck on my tongue and between my teeth.

Erik grabs a fistful of dried leaves and throws it at me. "Stupid dog," he mutters. He stands up, brushes himself off, and walks away.

"No need to call names," I say.

I look down at Rufus. He's got a bone-shaped tag like mine, except his is on a long chain of beads that's looped around his neck. Mine is on my collar. I think the words on his tag say "My name is Rufus."

I pick Rufus up by the tail (there's no glitter on his tail!) and trot him back to Adara.

"Yay. Buddy got your dog back," Jemma says.

Adara wrinkles her nose as she takes Rufus from me. "Yeah, but now Rufus has dog germs on him." She wipes her dog on the grass.

"Dog germs on your dog. That's funny," Connor says.

Adara scowls at Connor. "Erik is so mean," she says.

"He can be," Caroline agrees.

Adara hugs her dog again. "Rufus is very special. My grandma gave him to me right before we moved."

"Why'd you bring him to school if he's so special?" Michael asks.

"Because we're having a Pet Pound in Mrs. Argus's room today," Adara says.

My ears pop straight up. Pet Pound? As

in the *P-O-U-N-D*? I don't like that word.

"What's a Pet Pound?" Connor asks. I *really* don't like it when Connor says that word.

"It's when we bring our favorite stuffed animals to school so we can read to them," Caroline explains. "Mrs. Argus says that from now on, every Wednesday is Pet Pound day."

"Stop saying that word!" I yowl. "You should never say *P-O-U-N-D*. You should only spell it!"

"What's the matter with Buddy?" Michael asks Connor.

Connor shrugs. "Maybe he doesn't want the kids in Mrs. Argus's class to read to stuffed animals instead of to him."

WHAT? The kids in Mrs. Argus's room are going to read to stuffed animals now instead of to ME?

"Do you know why Mrs. Argus started the Pet Pound?" Jemma says.

"Why?" Connor asks.

"So she can take a nap while we're busy reading to our pets," Jemma says.

The girls giggle.

"Huh?" Michael says. "What are you talking about?"

"Mrs. Argus is very tired," Caroline says.

Adara nods. "She fell asleep during silent reading yesterday."

"I think she fell asleep on Monday, too. I bet that's why she forgot to come pick us up after music," Jemma says.

"She's been acting very weird lately," Caroline says.

Hmm. I'd better keep an eye on Mrs. Argus. Adara and the other first-graders' safety could be in my paws!

2

Escape

I have a problem. I can't keep an eye on Mrs. Argus, because I'm stuck in Mom's office. Her door is open, but there's a gate stretched across the doorway.

"Excuse me?" I say to Mom. "Would you mind moving the gate?"

Mom is the alpha human at this school. Alpha humans do important things on the computer. They don't pay a lot of attention to the dog.

I could jump over the gate, but Ellie would probably catch me. Ellie is second in command of the school. Her desk is on the other side of the gate. As soon as she catches me, she and Mom will call me Bad Dog. I don't like it when humans call me Bad Dog.

Maybe I'll just stand here and wait for someone to take the gate away.

I'm waiting…

…and waiting…

Still waiting…

Hey, what's that smell?

Liver treats! I LOVE liver treats. They're my favorite food! Ellie has a brand-new bag of them on her desk.

I stare at Ellie. "Can I have a treat?" I ask. Here's a secret: You're more likely to get a treat if you ask with your eyes instead of your mouth.

Ellie glances over at me and smiles. I don't think she knows what I'm asking.

"Treat! Treat! Treat! Treat! Treat!" I say with my eyes.

Now Ellie is writing on some papers on her desk. She's not even looking at me.

I rest my chin on the top of the gate. "I know you're busy. All you have to do is open the bag, grab a treat, and throw it to me.

Please? It won't take long."

Ellie turns to her computer.

I sigh. I don't think I'm going to get a treat anytime soon. And I can't go check on Mrs. Argus. So I go over to my pillow, turn a circle, and plop down.

"Wake me if you've got a job for me to do," I tell Mom. Then I rest my head on my paws and dream about liver treats… and chicken treats…and beef treats…I am rolling in all kinds of treats. I LOVE this dream! I could stay in this dream forever.

But I pop awake when Mom gets up from her computer. She's walking to the door. *She's going to move the gate!*

Aw, she only moves it far enough so she can leave her office. Then she slides it back into place. Her feet go click-click-click down the hallway.

My tail droops.

"Don't worry, Buddy," Ellie says. "She'll be back soon."

I'm not worried about Mom. I'm worried about Adara and the other kids in Mrs. Argus's class.

Now *Ellie* is getting up from her desk. She's walking into the bathroom.

I'm alone in the office!

Here's my chance! I back up to get a running start, hop over the gate, and dart out of the office.

There's no one in the hallway. All the teachers and kids are busy in their classrooms.

I go around the corner and down the hall to Mrs. Argus's room. I stop right outside the door and listen. It's quiet in there. I slooowly peek around the corner.

All the kids are working hard at their desks. Mrs. Argus is stapling papers to a wall. She's awake. It looks like the first-graders are safe. For now.

"Hi, Buddy," a boy named Zack whispers, waving at me. Zack and I are old friends. He was involved in a case I solved eleventy-ten days ago.

I want to tell him "Shhh!" because I don't want Mrs. Argus to see me. But my mouth doesn't go "Shhh!"

Hey, look at all those animals lined up on the counter by the open windows. I go over to check them out. They're not real animals. They're stuffed animals. I see a giraffe. A monkey. An elephant. Adara's dog, Rufus, is propped up between a hedgehog and a bear.

I have a bear at Connor's house. I LOVE my bear. He's my favorite toy! Do you know what I love about my bear? You can bite down on any of his paws or his tummy and he'll make a wonderful squeaky sound. I wonder if the bear on the counter makes squeaky sounds?

"Mrs. Argus!" Adara says as air from the open window ruffles the fur on my ears. "Buddy is trying to steal our Pound Pets."

Mrs. Argus looks at me with mad eyes.

"What? No, I'm not," I say as Mrs. Argus walks over to me. "I just want to see if the bear squeaks."

But before I can find out, the box on the wall crackles and Ellie's voice comes out of that box. "May I have your attention, please? Buddy seems to have escaped from Mrs. Keene's office." People at school call Mom Mrs. Keene.

Everyone in Mrs. Argus's class is looking at me. A few kids giggle.

"If he's in your classroom right now, would you please buzz the office?" Ellie says.

Mrs. Argus goes right to her telephone and tattles on me.

Here is what I know about tattling:

🐾 There is good tattling.

🐾 There is bad tattling.

Good tattling is when you want to get someone out of trouble. Bad tattling is when you want to get someone into trouble.

I think Mrs. Argus is trying to get me into trouble. That's BAD tattling. I am OUT OF HERE!!!!

I dash out into the hall and OOF! Mrs. Warner grabs me around the middle before I even smell her coming!

"There you are, Buddy," she says.

I wag my tail. I LOVE Mrs. Warner.

Mrs. Warner holds me by my collar and pokes her head into Mrs. Argus's room. "Would you tell Mrs. Keene that I've got Buddy?" she says. "I've got several kids signed up to read with him this morning, so I'll just take him to the library."

Oh, boy! The library! I LOVE the library. It's my favorite place!

3

Rufus Is Missing

Mrs. Warner is the boss of the library. Just like Mom is the boss of the school. Don't tell Mrs. Warner ("Shhh!"), but I don't know how to read.

I don't think you have to know how to read if you want to be a therapy dog. You just have to be a good listener. And you should probably like books.

I'm a very good listener. And I LOVE books.

Today a girl named Sabra reads to me about a pigeon who wants to drive a bus. I LOVE that book. It's my favorite book!

Then a boy named Skyler reads to me about a dog who enters an art contest. I LOVE that book. It's my favorite book!

And a boy named Cael reads to me about a man with one leg who rides a bike across a country in Africa. I LOVE that book. It's my favorite book!

Do you see why I LOVE being a therapy dog?

"Okay, Buddy," Mrs. Warner says. "Time to go back to the office."

"Awwwwww," I say. I wish kids could read to me forever and ever and ever and ever and ever.

But they can't.

We pass Mrs. Argus's room again on the way to the office. I hear a lot of noise and excitement coming from that room.

It's not the good kind of excitement.

Oh, no. There's water running down Adara's cheeks.

"What's the matter, Adara?" I ask, trotting over to her. Mrs. Warner is holding my leash, so she comes, too.

Adara turns her back to me while Jemma rubs her back.

"What's going on, Mrs. Argus?" Mrs. Warner asks.

"We just got back from P.E. and found Adara's dog is missing from our Pet Pound," Mrs. Argus says.

I go over to the counter, where all the stuffed animals are lined up. I see the bear…the hedgehog…the giraffe…and all the other animals. I don't see Rufus.

"He was in the Pet Pound before we went

to P.E.," Adara cries. "I petted him when I got in line. But he's not there now."

Sniff…sniff…sniff…I may not see Rufus, but I smell his scent: apples, paint, glitter, and pillow stuffing. I remember it from when I grabbed him this morning. I try to follow the scent, but it's hard. There are eleventy-twelve other scents in this room right now.

Rufus, I tell my nose. *Find Rufus*. I sniff under desks. I sniff the craft area. I sniff the reading area.

No Rufus.

Adara wipes her face on her arm. "I think someone stole him while we were at P.E.," she says with a sniff.

"Oh, I don't think so," Mrs. Argus says. "I was here the whole time you were gone."

I scamper over to Mrs. Argus's desk. I sniff under her desk. Hey, there's popcorn under there! I LOVE popcorn. It's my favorite food! I gobble up one…two…five… three…nine pieces of popcorn.

"You weren't in here when you walked us to P.E.," Zack says to Mrs. Argus.

"Or when you came to get us," Caroline adds.

"Well, that's true," Mrs. Argus says. "But I don't know who would've come in and taken your dog."

"Someone who wanted him," Adara says.

I check Mrs. Argus's garbage can. I don't

see Rufus in there. But I do see an empty Chinese-food carton. Maybe that's a clue.

Sniff…sniff…I smell lo mein. I LOVE lo mein. It's my favorite food! There's a noodle stuck to the side of the carton. I slurp it up.

Uh-oh. I feel a hand on my collar. "Stay out of my garbage," Mrs. Argus warns as she pulls me out from under her desk.

"Sorry," I say. But sometimes a dog can't help himself.

Wait a minute. "Let me sniff your hand again," I say to Mrs. Argus. I think I smelled Rufus's scent on Mrs. Argus's hand.

But she won't let me sniff it again. She holds her hand far out of my reach.

Four paws on the floor, I remind myself. I don't want to accidentally jump up and sniff her hand. Only Bad Dogs jump up, and I am not a Bad Dog.

I dig my paws into the floor. "Did you take Rufus?" I ask Mrs. Argus.

She doesn't answer me.

"Did you take Rufus to a Chinese restaurant?" I ask.

She still doesn't answer.

Adara makes mad eyes at Erik. "I bet you took my Rufus," she says.

"I did not!" Erik stomps his foot.

"You took him before," Jemma says. "On the way to school."

"That doesn't mean I took him now," Erik says. "When could I have taken him?"

"During P.E.," Adara says.

"You did leave P.E. for a little bit," Zack points out.

"To go to the bathroom!" Erik throws his hands into the air.

"Erik didn't take your dog, Adara," Mrs. Argus says. But I don't know how she can know that for sure.

I remember what those girls said on the way to school this morning: Mrs. Argus has been falling asleep in school. If she fell asleep while her students were at P.E., anyone could have come in and taken Rufus.

"Did you fall asleep while everyone was gone?" I ask Mrs. Argus.

I get the feeling Mrs. Argus understands my questions. She just doesn't want to answer them. I will have to find another way to solve this mystery.

I go over to Erik and give him a good sniff. I smell Rufus, but do you know what? I think it's a leftover smell from earlier this morning. I also smell soap from the bathroom. The soap scent is stronger than Rufus's scent.

Erik shoves me away and my face bumps into the girl behind him. Now, she smells interesting.

Sniff…sniff…She's got a tiny bit of Rufus's scent on her, but there's another scent, too. A stronger scent. It's sweat. And FEAR.

I rest my head on her leg. "What are you afraid of?" I ask with my eyes. This girl has never read to me in the library, so I don't know her name.

She scratches my ears and, *oh*, she's got wonderful fingernails! It feels so, so good when she scratches me.

Then she clears her throat and says, "Buddy likes stuffed animals. Maybe *he* came in when no one else was here and took Adara's dog."

Everyone looks at me. They're looking at me like they think I'm a Bad Dog.

"I didn't!" I say. "I wouldn't take someone else's dog. I got Rufus back when Erik took him earlier today. Remember, Adara? Caroline? Jemma?"

None of them defend me.

Finally, Mrs. Warner says, "Buddy couldn't have taken Adara's dog, Maddy. Not if he disappeared while you were at P.E. Buddy has been with me in the library for the last couple of hours."

I wag my tail. "Thanks, Mrs. Warner," I say.

But even though Mrs. Warner gave me an alibi, Adara and Mrs. Argus are still looking at me like they think I'm a Bad Dog. They think I took Rufus.

4

On the Trail

I have to find Rufus. Not just because I want Adara to like me. I need to show everyone I'm not a Bad Dog. Or a thief.

I curl up on my pillow in Mom's office and think about this case. Here is what I KNOW:

- 🐾 I didn't take Rufus.

- 🐾 Rufus was last seen in the Pet P-O-U-N-D in Mrs. Argus's room.

- 🐾 He was last seen right before the kids went to P.E.

- 🐾 The P-O-U-N-D Pets were alone when Mrs. Argus took the kids to P.E.

❧ Mrs. Argus came back to the room while her kids were at P.E.

❧ She did not see anyone take Rufus.

❧ The P-O-U-N-D Pets were alone when Mrs. Argus went to get the kids from P.E.

Here is what I DON'T KNOW:

❧ Did someone come in to Mrs. Argus's room when the P-O-U-N-D Pets were alone?

❧ Did Mrs. Argus fall asleep while the kids were at P.E.?

❧ Did someone take Rufus?

❧ Could Rufus have disappeared some other way?

Here is my PLAN for solving this case:

🐾 ???

"Time for recess, Buddy," Mom says.

Recess? I LOVE recess. It's my favorite thing! Maybe a little fresh air will help me figure out a plan to solve this case.

Mom takes me out to the playground and unhooks my leash. FREEDOM!

I run and run and run! Some kids try to

chase me, but I'm too fast for them. While I'm running, I see a lady pushing a boy in a stroller across the playground.

I see Erik run past Adara and pull her hair. I bark at him because he isn't being very nice.

Then I see the girl with the wonderful fingernails, the one who said maybe *I* stole Rufus. Mrs. Warner called her Maddy. Maddy is sitting by herself with her back against the wall of the school and her head on her knees.

I slink over to her.

Another girl from Mrs. Argus's class comes over, too. She sits down beside Maddy and asks, "What's wrong?" I think this girl's name is Deepa.

Water rolls down Maddy's cheeks. I lean over and lick the water from her cheek. Mm. Salty.

I lie down and put my head on Maddy's leg. She and Deepa both pet me.

Maddy sniffs and wipes her cheek. "If I

tell you, do you promise not to tell anyone?" she asks.

"Okay," Deepa says.

Maddy leans close to Deepa and whispers, "You know Adara's dog, Rufus?"

Deepa nods.

More water runs down Maddy's cheeks. "I accidentally knocked him out the window when we were lining up for P.E."

My ears pop up. That's why I smelled fear on her. Is that why she wanted everyone to think I took Rufus? So they wouldn't think *she* did it?

Deepa's eyes open wide. "Why didn't you tell Mrs. Argus?" she asks.

"I was afraid she'd get mad," Maddy says. "I was afraid Adara would get mad, too, and not like me anymore."

I lick Maddy's hand to show her I understand.

"I also thought he'd still be here when we came out for recess," Maddy goes on. "I was going to find him and give him back to Adara. But he's not here. I don't know where he is."

"Let's all use our noses and see if we can find him," I say, hopping to my feet.

Sniff...sniff...What's that in the grass? It's glitter! Glitter from Rufus's shirt. That means Rufus *was* here.

But we already knew that.

Sniff...sniff...I think I smell a trail of apples, paint, glitter, and pillow stuffing. That's Rufus's trail!

"Maybe one of the big kids found him during their recess and turned him in to the Lost and Found?" Deepa says.

"Do you think so?" Maddy asks.

"Let's go see," Deepa says.

The girls get up and run toward Mrs. Argus, who is standing near the front door. I want to follow them. I want to see if Rufus is in the Lost and Found.

But I also want to follow Rufus's trail.

I don't know what to do.

Rufus's trail is never going to be as fresh as it is right now. I follow the trail!

Sniff...sniff...The trail takes me across the blacktop...under the climbing structure...and over to where a bunch of older kids are playing soccer. I LOVE soccer! It's my favorite game.

"Hi, Buddy," Alex says as I trot along

beside him. I met Alex five thousand days ago when Connor, Michael, and Jillian followed a trail of their own and found out about a secret club at this school. Alex was in the club. Now Connor, Michael, and Jillian are in it, too.

Alex stops for a second to pet me. Hey, is it my imagination or do I smell Rufus's scent on him?

And what's that on his hand? Glitter? Yes! In fact, it's the same glitter that was on Rufus's shirt.

That's weird. Alex is a fourth-grader. He's a friend of Connor's, but he doesn't live on our street. He didn't walk to school with us. I'm not sure he even knows Adara.

So why do I smell Rufus's scent on him? And why is there glitter from Rufus's shirt on his hand?

Someone kicks the ball to Alex, and he zooms away with it.

Alex doesn't have Rufus with him now. I

look around. I don't see Rufus anywhere on the playground.

But I still smell his trail.

I follow the trail across the soccer field and over to a gate in the chain-link fence.

Sniff...sniff...I'm pretty sure the trail continues on the other side of that gate. How am I going to get over there?

5

The Chase Is On

I try to nudge the gate open with my nose. It doesn't budge.

I can't jump over the fence. It's too tall.

I can't dig under it. The ground is too hard.

I need help from a human. I scan the playground for someone who might help. I see a girl reading a book under a tree. I don't know her, but I run to her anyway.

"Would you please open that gate for me?" I ask. "I'm on a very important case. I'm trying to find a missing **P-O-U-N-D** Pet."

She keeps on reading.

I rest my chin on the top of her book. "Pleeeeease, will you open the gate?" I ask with my eyes.

She pats my head, then turns away.

She's not going to help me.

I look around for someone else who might help. I see Jaden standing by the climbing structure. Jaden is a fourth-grader who's read to me five or three times. I run to him. "Will you open the gate for me?" I ask.

He jumps up and grabs one of the bars above his head. I leap back out of the way so he doesn't kick me as he walks across the bars with his hands.

I sigh. He's not going to help me, either.

Then I see Connor tossing a tennis ball from one hand to the other. Oh, I LOVE tennis balls. They're my favorite things!

Connor sees me, too. "Do you want to play Fetch, Buddy?" he asks.

My tail wags all by itself. "I would LOVE to—wait, NO! I can't. I'm busy following Rufus's trail. I need someone to open that gate for me. Will you open it?" I turn so he knows what gate I'm talking about.

Connor doesn't even look at the gate. He

throws the tennis ball so it bounces right in front of me, and I can't stop myself from chasing it...right into the middle of the soccer game.

Alex kicks the soccer ball and Michael leaps up and bounces it off his head. The soccer ball sails toward the fence.

Hey! That gives me an idea!

I race after the soccer ball. So do a bunch of other kids. A boy named Quinn gets to it first. He gives it a good kick and I block it.

"No, Buddy!" a bunch of kids shout. "Get out of our game!"

"Yay! Buddy's on our team!" Michael yells.

"I'm not on anyone's team," I say. I try to get my nose under the ball, but Alex steals it away from me.

Alex dribbles the ball with his feet, then gives it a good kick. A girl I don't know blocks it and kicks it back toward me. This time I can get under it and pop it up with my nose. The ball hits the top of the fence and bounces back toward us. Darn. Not quite high enough.

I dash up and down the field with the kids. Every time the ball goes high, I try to hit it over the fence with my nose. But I can never hit it quite right.

This may not work after all.

I'm about to give up when the ball comes sailing toward me in just the right arc. I jump up and pop the ball over the fence.

Hooray! Now someone will have to go get it.

"I'll get the ball," Quinn says. He jogs over to the gate. I trot along beside him. As soon as the gate starts to open, I crowd in and push my way through.

Ugh! I'm stuck.

Wait, no I'm not. My collar was stuck, but it sprang from my neck. Now it's hanging from the gate. And I'm FREE! Free to follow Rufus's trail.

Kids yell behind me: "BUDDY!"... "Oh, no! Buddy's loose! Someone get him!"... "You guys! We can't leave school! We'll get in trouble!"..."We have to tell a teacher. Buddy's loose!"

I hear Connor's voice: "I'll go tell my mom."

"Don't worry," I call over my shoulder. "I'll come back as soon as I find Rufus!"

I follow Rufus's trail down the street and around a corner. There's a man standing on the sidewalk. He puts his phone to his ear and says something about a loose dog as I rush past.

I round another corner, my ears flapping in the wind. Hey, what's that shiny thing on the sidewalk up ahead?

It's a bone-shaped dog tag. It's not attached to a dog collar. It's attached to a chain of beads.

Sniff…sniff…It's Rufus's dog tag!

I grab the chain in my mouth and look up at the house in front of me. Is Rufus in

there?

All of a sudden, a strange metal object pulls at my neck. It's not a collar—it's some sort of ring that's attached to a long metal pole.

"Gotcha!" a man at the other end of the pole yells.

I'm so startled I almost drop the chain. But I grip it tight between my teeth as the man uses the pole to pull me toward a van that's parked at the curb.

Uh-oh. What's happening?

The man opens the back door of the van, shoves me in, and slams the door in my face.

I spit out the chain. *Where am I?*

There are wire bars all around me. I'm in some sort of cage. A cage in the back of a strange van.

I scratch at the bars. "Let me out!" I cry.

The man opens the middle door of the van and lays the long pole inside. Then he slams the door closed and climbs into the front seat.

"I don't know you," I say. "I don't want to go with you. STRANGER DANGER! STRANGER DANGER!"

The man starts driving.

"WHERE ARE YOU TAKING ME!" I demand, scratching at the bars some more.

"Shut up back there!" the man says.

I don't like this man.

We drive for a long, long, long, long time. Finally, we turn into a parking lot in front of a small brick building.

Gulp! I know this place.

This is the **P-O-U-N-D**. And I'm not talking about the **P-O-U-N-D** in Mrs. Argus's room. This is the *real* **P-O-U-N-D**.

6

Bad Dog!

The man drives into a big garage and the garage door goes down behind us. He gets out of the van, walks around to the back, and opens my door.

I back away. I can hear other dogs talking in the distance: "Where are my people?"..."I don't like it here!"..."I want to go home!"

"Come on," the man says. He grabs me by the scruff of my neck and drags me out of the van. I dart away and run to the far corner of the garage.

There's got to be a way out of here, but I don't see one. The only open door leads inside the P-O-U-N-D.

"A little help out here, please?" the man

calls. "I've got a loose dog." But I don't think anyone inside the **P-O-U-N-D** can hear him.

The man opens the middle door of the van and brings out that long pole. As he moves toward me with that pole, I race to the other side of the van and he starts chasing me. Round and round the van.

The third time around, I spot Rufus's dog tag. It's still in the back of the van. I hop up, grab it with my teeth, and hop back down again. But before I can dart away, I feel that metal ring go around my neck again and the bad man drags me across the garage, through the door, and into the **P-O-U-N-D**.

A lady comes out of a back room to greet us. "Well, hello," she says, smiling at me. "Who do we have here?"

I don't think I've met her before. She smells like a bean-and-cheese burrito. I LOVE bean-and-cheese burritos. They're my favorite food!

51

The man lets me go. "Don't know," he says. "I found him running loose on Grant Street. He doesn't have any tags."

Burrito Lady gets down on one knee beside me. "He's got a tag," she says, rubbing my back. "He's carrying it in his mouth."

The man comes over and yanks the chain out from between my teeth.

"Hey!" I cry out.

I jump up to try to get Rufus's tag back, but the man hands it to Burrito Lady. "Not very helpful," he says. "There's no contact information."

Burrito Lady reads the words on the tag out loud. "'I belong to Adara.'"

Oh. Is that what it says?

"Who's Adara?" Burrito Lady asks me. "Is she your mom?"

"No. She's my neighbor," I say. "And that tag belongs to her very special stuffed dog, Rufus. I need it back so I can find him.

Please can I have it back?"

Burrito Lady has no idea what I'm saying. "Don't worry. We'll find Adara," she says to me. She lays the tag on the counter, then turns to the man. "Thanks for bringing him in."

"No problem." He tips his hat, then leaves. I am not sorry to see him go.

Burrito Lady grabs a collar and leash

from a basket on a shelf and puts them on me. Then she leads me into a small room with a table in the middle. "Let's find out if you're microchipped," she says.

"I am!" I tell her. Mom got me microchipped soon after I went to live with her and Connor.

Burrito Lady picks up a scanner and runs it over the back of my neck. "Aha!" she says. "You do have a chip. That means we can find your people." She grabs a pad of paper and writes down some numbers. "Handsome boy like you? I bet they'll rush right over to pick you up."

I hope so. I need to get back to my case.

"Let's go find you a nice kennel while you wait." Burrito Lady walks me into the big room with all the kennels.

All the dogs in there start talking at once: "Hello? Who's this?" "Don't put him in my kennel. This is my kennel. MY KENNEL!" "Where are my people? Are my people ever coming to get me?" "I hate this place!" "King? Is that you, King?"

I whirl around. My name used to be King. Back when I lived with Kayla.

"George!" I cry, pulling toward the bulldog. George and I are old friends. "How are you?"

"I'm all right," George replies. "The hip is giving me trouble, but I'm all right."

"I can't believe you're still here," I say. "Haven't you found a new family to adopt?"

"Nah," George says. "Not yet."

I'm worried about George. If he doesn't choose a new family soon—I don't want to think about it.

"What are you doing back here?" George asks me. "Didn't your new family work out?"

"No, they're working out great—HEY!" Burrito Lady practically yanks me off my feet.

"Come along, Mister," she says. "You

don't need to bark at all these other dogs."

"My name's not Mister," I tell her. "And I'm not *barking*."

"Yeah, we're just talking. We're trying to catch up," George puts in.

Burrito Lady leads me through another door into a whole new part of the P-O-U-N-D. A part I've never been to before. They have kennels in here, too. But not as many as in the other room. And there are no other dogs back here.

Uh-oh. I think I know what this place is: Solitary Confinement.

Burrito Lady unclips my leash, opens one of the kennels, and nudges me inside. Then she turns out the light and closes the door on her way out.

I'm all alone.

I groan. Solitary is as bad as everyone said it was. No one to talk to. Nothing to look at. Just a bowl of stale kibble. A bowl of water. And darkness all around me.

I turn a circle in my cage and lie down. I hope Mom and Connor come for me soon.

I don't think Mom and Connor are ever coming for me. I'll be stuck here forever. FOREVER!

I've already been here forever. With no one to talk to. Nothing to play with.

I'll never see Mom or Connor or anyone else ever again.

I'll never run and play in my yard…never see Mouse again…never find Rufus…never solve another mystery. There are so many things I'll never do again that I start to make a list of them inside my head:

🐾 Never listen to kids read to me

🐾 Never enjoy a real meal

🐾 Never chase Cat with No Name

Finally, the door opens and the light comes on. Burrito Lady is back! "Your mom is here, Buddy," she says cheerfully.

"Hey, you know my name now," I say as she opens my kennel and snaps a leash to my collar.

But I still don't know her name.

As we walk back through the big room with all the kennels, all the dogs start talking again: "Where's he going?"..."How come he gets to go outside?"..."Where are you going, King?"

"The name's Buddy now," I tell George. "And I'm going home!"

"Good for you, Buddy," George says. "Good for you."

Burrito Lady opens another door and Mom runs to me. "Oh, Buddy," she says, hugging me. "Why do you keep running off like this?"

"I was trying to find Rufus—" I start to explain.

"I almost forgot," Burrito Lady says. She goes behind the counter and gets the chain with Rufus's tag. "He had this in his mouth when he came in. I assume Adara is your daughter?"

Mom takes the chain. She's got my collar sticking out of a pocket in her purse. "No, Adara is our neighbor," she says, taking a closer look at the tag. "Did you say Buddy had this in his mouth?"

"Yes."

"Did he have a stuffed animal with him, too?"

"No. Just this," Burrito Lady says.

"Oh." Mom groans. "Some kids at school told me Adara's stuffed dog got knocked out of her classroom window this morning. And now he's missing. He was wearing a little dog tag that says, 'I belong to Adara.'"

"That must be the tag," Burrito Lady says.

"Must be," Mom says. She looks at me

59

with mad eyes. "Did you find Rufus, Buddy? What did you do with him?"

"Nothing," I say. "I didn't find him. I—"

"You've been a very Bad Dog today, Buddy," Mom interrupts me. "You took Adara's dog. You ran away. What are we going to do with you?"

I hang my head. I don't like it when people think I'm a Bad Dog. Especially when I'm trying so hard to be a Good Dog.

But I'm going to find Rufus and clear my name. Really, I am!

7

Visiting Mouse

Mom puts me in the back seat of the car. I LOVE the car. It's my favorite thing.

"Where are we going?" I ask. "Back to school?" I pace back and forth along the seat.

"Settle down, Buddy," Mom says as she starts the car. She doesn't tell me where we're going. She just drives. She doesn't even open my window so I can feel the breeze on my face and smell all the wonderful outdoor smells.

I sit tall in the middle of the back seat and watch the road through the front window. This is not the way to school.

But it is the way home! I wag my tail. "Are we going home!" I ask. "Is school out?" It must be. I was at the **P-O-U-N-D** a long,

long, LONG time!

Mom turns onto our street, then stops the car in the middle of the road. "Oh, no," she says.

"What?" I say, looking all around. Does she see Cat with No Name? I don't see or smell him. But he could be lurking somewhere around here.

Mom starts driving again. She drives right on past our house and stops in front of Michael's house. Connor is in the driveway playing basketball with Michael.

Both boys turn and run toward the car. "You found him!" Connor cries. "You found Buddy."

Mom rolls down her window, but she *still* doesn't roll down mine. "Yes," she says. "Someone picked him up and took him to the animal shelter."

"Good thing we got him microchipped," Connor says.

I stick my head out Mom's window and

Connor scratches my ear.

"I've got a meeting downtown," Mom says. "I was hoping to drop Buddy off at home. But the cleaning lady is still there, and she doesn't like dogs."

I look out the back window and see the strange car in our driveway.

"You can leave Buddy here with us, Mrs. K," Michael says. "We can put him in the backyard with Mouse."

Oh, yay! I wag my tail. I love to hang with Mouse!

"Are you sure?" Mom asks. "Maybe we should ask your parents." Michael's parents have only been his parents for three or eleven months. They got adopted by both Mouse *and* Michael.

"They won't mind," Michael says. "I know they won't." He opens my door and Connor grabs my leash as I hop out.

"Okay. If you're sure," Mom says. "Thanks, boys!" She waves, then drives away.

Connor and Michael lead me over to the gate that goes to Mouse's backyard. They open the gate and unhook my leash. Then they close the gate really fast and go back to their game.

Mouse looks up from inside his doghouse. "BUDDY! HI!" he says, trotting over to greet me. We sniff each other.

"WHAT'S WRONG?" Mouse asks. "YOU SMELL LIKE YOU HAVE A PROBLEM." He sniffs me some more, then gasps. "Y–Y–YOU SMELL LIKE THE *P-O-U-N-D*! WERE YOU AT THE *P-O-U-N-D*?"

"Yes," I say. I tell Mouse the whole story. I tell him about Adara's dog, Rufus, and how he went missing. I tell him about Maddy accidentally knocking Rufus out the window and about how I tracked his scent across the playground and away from the school. I tell him about the strange man who grabbed me and took me to the *P-O-U-N-D*. And I tell him that now everyone thinks *I* took Rufus.

"I have to find that stuffed dog," I say when I finally get to the end of the story.

"HOW ARE YOU GOING TO DO THAT?" Mouse asks.

"I don't know," I say. I drop to my belly. "Do you have any ideas?"

"Not really," Mouse says.

We watch our people shoot baskets. And I am thinking, thinking, thinking about what I should do next. I hope Mouse is thinking, too.

"Maybe I should go back to where I found Rufus's tag and see if I can track him from there," I say.

"THAT SOUNDS DANGEROUS," Mouse says. "WHAT IF SOMEONE ELSE PICKS YOU UP AND TAKES YOU BACK TO THE P-O-U-N-D?"

"Then Burrito Lady will call Mom and she'll come get me. Just like before," I say.

"WHAT IF BURRITO LADY ISN'T

THERE ANYMORE?" Mouse asks.

"Well...I've got a chip in my neck," I remind Mouse. "Whoever is there will find it and call Mom." I've got to find Rufus, and this is my best plan. My only plan. I hop to my feet and scan Mouse's backyard for a way out. The dirt around the back fence looks pretty loose. I could probably dig my way under the fence.

"Help me dig!" I tell Mouse as I race across the yard.

"BUDDY, NO!" Mouse cries, chasing after me. "WE CAN'T DIG UNDER THE FENCE! WE'LL GET IN TROUBLE!"

"No, we won't," I say. I'm already digging. "Our people are busy playing basketball. I can go back to where I found Rufus's tag, search for Rufus, and be back before Connor even knows I'm gone."

"WHAT ABOUT THE HOLE IN MY YARD?" Mouse asks. "WE'LL GET IN TROUBLE FOR DIGGING!"

"No one will know *we* dug it," I say.

"THEY MAY NOT KNOW *YOU* DUG IT, BUT MY PEOPLE WILL KNOW *I* DUG IT," Mouse says. "AND I'LL BE IN TROUBLE WITH MY PEOPLE!"

"Oh," I say. I don't want Mouse to get in trouble with his people.

"Why are the dogs barking?" Connor asks. The other boys all

turn to look at Mouse and me.

I quickly push a little of the dirt back into the hole.

"Hey, guys!" Two boys cross the street and walk over to Connor and Michael. It's Alex and Quinn from school. "Can we play?" Quinn asks.

"Sure," Connor says, tossing the ball to him.

"Now we know why the dogs were barking," Michael says. "They were letting us know you guys were here."

Mouse and I look at each other. Our people try to understand what we're saying, but it's hard for them.

"Is that Buddy from school?" Alex points at me.

"Yeah," Michael says. "He and my dog are friends."

The boys come over to the fence. "Hi, Buddy," Alex says, reaching over to pet me. But he can't quite reach.

If I'm not going to dig my way out, I may as well get petted. Mouse and I inch closer.

I still smell Rufus's scent on Alex! It's not as strong as it was before, but it's still there.

Alex moves down the fence so he can pet Mouse. "What's your dog's name?" he asks Michael.

"Mouse."

"Mouse?" Alex laughs. "That dog doesn't look much like a mouse."

Michael shrugs. "I know. My foster parents named him before I got here."

"Sniff Alex," I tell Mouse. "Give him a really good sniff. Do you smell what I smell?"

Mouse sniffs. "BESIDES ALEX'S

NORMAL SMELL, I SMELL PAINT AND
PILLOWS AND—" he says.

"That's Rufus's scent," I say.

The boys all give Mouse and me
one more pat, then they return to their
basketball game.

"WHY DOES ALEX HAVE RUFUS'S
SCENT ON HIM? DID *HE* TAKE
RUFUS?" Mouse asks.

"Maybe," I say. "Maybe he found Rufus
when he went out for recess. But instead of
taking him into the school, he took him to
his house."

"IN THE MIDDLE OF RECESS?"
Mouse asks.

I agree that seems strange. I don't know
if he had time to do all that. But here's one
thing I do know: Alex has Rufus's scent
on him. Mouse smelled it, too. And here's
another thing I know: I found Rufus's dog
tag away from school property. And I found
it when all the kids were at school.

"Time to go home, Buddy," Connor says after a little while. He comes into the backyard and clips my leash to my collar.

"See you guys tomorrow!" Alex waves, then heads down the street.

I wonder where he's going. I bet he's going home.

"MAYBE YOU AND CONNOR CAN FOLLOW ALEX AND SEE IF HE'S GOT RUFUS AT HIS HOUSE," Mouse says.

"That's what I was thinking," I tell Mouse. "Come on, Connor. Let's go with Alex."

I can't tell whether Connor didn't hear me or he's ignoring me on purpose. But instead of following Alex, he starts walking in the opposite direction.

I dig in my paws. "We need to follow Alex," I say.

Connor gives my leash a gentle tug. "This way, Buddy," he says.

"Well, fine. If you don't want to follow Alex, I'll go by myself." I try to pull my leash out of Connor's hand, but my boy is getting stronger.

"Oh, no you don't," he says, holding tight to my leash. "You're not getting away this

time. We're going home!"

"That's what you think," I say. I pull harder. HARDER!

Connor can't hold on.

Finally, I'm FREE!

"GOOD LUCK, BUDDY!" Mouse calls after me.

8

I Didn't Do It

"ALEX!" Connor yells behind me. "Buddy's loose. Can you catch him?"

Alex turns. He reaches for me, but I dart out of the way.

Connor, Michael, and Quinn run up behind us. Now they're all trying to catch me.

I turn and leap away every time.

"I'm not going to let you catch me," I tell the boys. "But I'll stay close to you if you lead us to your house, Alex."

"Hey, Keene," Alex says to Connor. "I think your dog wants to come home with me, not you."

"Yes! That's right," I tell Connor with my tail. "But don't worry. I'm not going to adopt

Alex. I just want to see if he's got Rufus. Then we can go home."

"Do you have a dog?" Connor asks Alex.

"Yeah. Why?" Alex asks.

"Because that's probably why Buddy wants to follow you," Connor says. "He can smell your dog on you. He probably wants to meet your dog."

Actually, I didn't notice that Alex has a dog. I was too busy trying not to get caught. But now that they've pointed it out, I can smell Alex's dog. It's a little one. A terrier of some kind.

"Do you want to bring him over to meet my dog?" Alex asks Connor. "I just live over there." He points to a brick apartment building across the street.

I stop. That's where Alex lives? That's not where I found Rufus's tag. We aren't even close to where I found that.

And I don't smell Rufus's scent anywhere around here. Except a little bit on Alex.

76

"Gotcha!" Connor says as he grabs my leash. He turns to Alex. "I don't want to reward Buddy for running away. Plus I'd have to ask my mom before going to your house. I'd better go home."

I don't know why Alex has Rufus's scent on him, but I don't think he has Rufus. I may as well go home with Connor. I'll meet Alex's dog another time.

"Okay," Alex says. He and Connor bump fists and we all go our separate ways.

Mom and Connor are having cheeseburgers for dinner. I LOVE cheeseburgers. They're my favorite food!

I'm having kibble for dinner. Just kibble.

Usually, Connor slips me some of his dinner under the table. But not tonight. I put my head in his lap to remind him I'm here.

"You've been a Bad Dog today, Buddy," he says as he pushes my face away.

"Yes, you have," Mom agrees.

My tail can't get any lower.

"Look at Adara," Mom says. "Look how sad she is."

I crawl out from under the table and go to the window. Adara is sitting on her swing, but she's not swinging. She's just staring at the ground.

"I feel terrible about Adara's dog," Mom says to Connor.

Me, too.

"I wish I knew what Buddy did with

Rufus," Mom says.

"I didn't do anything with him," I say. "I never had him!"

"He probably hid him," Connor says as he pops the last bit of cheeseburger into his mouth. "Buddy always hides stuff that he really likes. Maybe we could go to school after dinner and see if we can find where he hid him."

"That's a good idea," Mom says, gazing out the window. "I wonder if Adara would like to come with us. Why don't you go ask her while I clear the table."

"Okay," Connor says. He heads for the back door and I follow a few steps behind.

"You stay here, Buddy," he says. He opens the door just enough so he can sneak out.

I groan. I trot back to the kitchen window and watch Connor run to the back fence. He and Adara talk for a little bit, then Adara runs into her house while Connor waits at the fence.

Mom bustles around our kitchen, putting away the ketchup, mustard, lettuce, cheese, and buns. Then she loads the dishes into the loud cleaning machine. I don't know why she doesn't let me clean the dishes. I can clean dishes as well as any cleaning machine. And I can do it a lot quieter.

Finally, the back door opens and Connor and Adara come in. I hurry over to greet them.

Adara backs away from me.

"Buddy!" Mom cries. "Leave Adara alone."

"What? I can't even say hello to her now?" I say. That doesn't seem very friendly.

"I'm so sorry Buddy took your dog, Adara," Mom says.

"I didn't take him," I tell Adara.

Mom gives Adara the chain with Rufus's dog tag. "Buddy had this when he arrived at the animal shelter," she says. "So we know he had Rufus at some point."

"No!" I say. "I only had his tag. I've been trying to find Rufus just like all of you!"

"Buddy! Stop barking. Lie down," Mom orders.

I drop to the floor. Why doesn't anyone understand?

"Are we ready to go?" Mom asks Adara and Connor.

"He's not coming with us. Is he?" Adara asks, pointing at me.

"No, he's not," Mom says.

Of course not. I put my head on my paws.

Then Connor says, "I think we should take Buddy with us. If he hid Rufus, maybe he'll show us where he hid him."

My head pops up. I didn't hide Rufus. But I might be able to find him. If they give me a chance.

Mom scratches her chin. "That's a good point, Connor," she says. "Adara, would it be okay if Buddy comes to school with us?

Connor can sit between you and Buddy. Connor could be right. We may need Buddy to help us find Rufus."

Adara thinks about it for eleventy-three minutes.

"Please let me come! Please let me come! Please let me come!" I beg with my eyes. But I don't stand up, because no one said I could stand up.

"Okay," Adara finally says.

HOORAY!!!! "Okay" is the word that means I can stand up. It also means I get to go in the car! I get to go to school! I get to help find Rufus!

Connor slides to the middle of the back seat. I sit on one side of him. Adara sits on the other. Then Mom drives us all to school.

It's starting to get dark outside. That's not a problem for me. My nose works just as well in the dark as it does in the light. But it might be a problem for Connor, Mom, and Adara.

Mom pulls in to her usual parking spot right by the door. There's a light on in one of the classrooms.

Connor sees the light, too. "Is someone else here?" he asks.

"I think that's Mrs. Argus's room," Mom says. "I wonder if she forgot to turn the light off."

Connor grabs my leash and we all get out of the car and walk toward the school. Mom opens her purse and pulls out a key. While she jiggles it into the lock, I press my ear against the door. That's strange. I hear music coming from inside the school.

Mom opens the door and we all rush in. We follow the sound of the music. It leads straight to Mrs. Argus's room.

Mrs. Argus is sitting at her computer type-type-typing away. She doesn't even notice us. I wonder what she's typing.

Mom clears her throat and Mrs. Argus jumps way up into the air. She presses a

button and her computer screen goes dark.

Mrs. Argus looks at each of us. She scowls at me. "You all scared me half to death," she says. "What are you doing here?"

"I think a better question is what are *you* doing here?" I ask.

9

Find Rufus

"We're here to see if we can find Adara's missing dog," Connor says.

"What are you doing here?" Mom asks Mrs. Argus.

Sniff...sniff...I still smell a tiny bit of Rufus's scent on Mrs. Argus. But there's another scent. A stronger scent. It's...a turkey sandwich. I LOVE turkey sandwiches! They're my favorite food.

There's something else, too. It's the same thing I smelled on Maddy: sweat... and FEAR. Did *Mrs. Argus* take Adara's dog? Is that why I smell fear on her?

"I'm, uh, working on my novel," Mrs. Argus says, not quite meeting Mom's gaze.

"Your novel?" Mom says with surprise.

"Yes. I'm writing a novel," Mrs. Argus says. She sounds a little embarrassed. "There's something wrong with my computer at home, so I've been bringing my dinner and working here every night. Sometimes until quite late, I'm afraid. I tend to lose track of time. I hope you don't mind."

So, *that's* why Mrs. Argus smells scared. She's afraid Mom will be mad at her for staying at school after everyone else has gone home.

It also explains why Mrs. Argus has been falling asleep in school. She's been staying up too late.

But it doesn't explain why she has Rufus's scent on her.

"How exciting that you're working on a novel," Mom says. "Of course you can stay at school to work. I hope you get your computer fixed soon."

"Thank you," Mrs. Argus says with a smile. It may be the first time I've ever seen her smile.

"Mrs. Argus?" Adara says, taking a step toward her teacher. "Do you know where Rufus is?"

"I wish I did, honey," Mrs. Argus says. "I also wish I'd closed the window when I arranged the animals in our Pet Pound."

So Mrs. Argus touched Rufus. That explains why I smell his scent on her.

"Yes, I understand one of your students accidentally knocked Rufus out the window this morning," Mom says. "I suspect Buddy picked him up during recess and hid him somewhere on the playground."

"Maddy knocked Rufus out the window. But I didn't pick him up. He was already gone by the time I got there," I say.

"Unfortunately, it's getting dark outside." Mom gazes out the window. "I don't know if we'll be able to find him in the dark."

"We're still going to try, aren't we?" Adara asks in a worried voice. "Rufus will be so scared alone in the dark."

"Of course we are," Mom says, patting her shoulder.

"I don't need light to find Rufus," I tell everyone. "I just need my nose. And someone to open the gate."

"I've got a flashlight, if that would help," Mrs. Argus says. She opens her desk drawer, takes out a flashlight, and hands it to Mom.

"Thank you," Mom says. Then we all go outside. Even Mrs. Argus!

"Okay, Buddy," Connor says, letting go of my leash. "Go find Rufus!"

I know right where I'm going. I race across the playground, and I don't stop until I get to the gate. Connor is almost as fast as I am, but it takes a long time for everyone else to catch up. Do we really have to wait for them?

"Open the gate," I tell Connor. "Please open the gate."

"I don't think Buddy understands what we want him to do," Mom says as she tries to catch her breath.

"Yes, I do!" I say, wagging my tail. "You want me to find Rufus."

"He might understand," Connor says. "He ran straight to the gate when I said, 'Find Rufus.' Maybe we should open the gate and see what he does next?"

"Yes! Open the gate!" I say.

"Well, okay," Mom says. "But grab his leash first."

Connor picks up my leash, then slowly opens the gate.

10

Real Dogs Are More Fun

We all rush through the gate and I lead everyone down the street. Sniff...sniff...I can still smell Rufus's scent, but it's not as strong as before.

"Where's Buddy going?" Adara calls from behind me and Connor.

"I don't know," Connor calls back. "I think he's following a trail."

"I am!" I say.

"Hopefully a trail will lead us to Rufus," Mom says.

We turn a corner and then I don't know where to go next. I've lost Rufus's scent!

Sniff...sniff...Where is it? It's got to be around here somewhere.

Maybe we weren't supposed to turn

onto this street. I whirl around and drag Connor—past Mom and Adara and Mrs. Argus—back to the corner.

Sniff...sniff...sniff...There are so many smells, and they're all mixing together inside my nose.

I glance back at Adara. "Could I please smell Rufus's tag?" I ask her.

She steps back. "Why is he barking at me?" she asks Mom.

"I'm not sure," Mom says. "But I don't think he's looking for Rufus. I think we should go back to school."

"No!" I say. "I'm looking for him. Really, I am."

"Not yet," Connor says. He turns to Adara. "Do you still have the tag Mom gave you? Maybe it would help if you let Buddy sniff that."

I wag my tail. My boy is so smart!

But Adara backs away from me.

"I'm not going to hurt you," I tell her. "I'm trying to help. But I need another sniff."

Adara reaches into her pocket and pulls out Rufus's tag. "Here. You let him sniff it," she says, handing it to Connor.

Connor holds the tag out to me and I take a good sniff. "Okay. I've got it now. We want to keep going straight," I tell everyone. We cross the street and then I see the house! The house from this morning.

I zoom toward it.

"Slow down, Buddy," Connor says. He's having a hard time holding on to my leash now.

I try to slow down, but it's hard when I'm excited. I just want to GET THERE AND FIND RUFUS! I drag Connor up the front steps and scratch at the door.

"Connor!" Mom calls from the sidewalk. "Don't let Buddy scratch on their door."

"I'm trying not to let him," Connor says as he pulls me back.

Mom, Adara, and Mrs. Argus finally catch up to us and I lunge for the door again. "HEY!" I yell. "DO YOU HAVE MY FRIEND

94

ADARA'S STUFFED DOG IN THERE?"

Connor rings the bell.

A light comes on over the front porch and the door opens. The lady in there is holding on to a little boy who's got part of his fist in his mouth. His other fist is clutching a stuffed dog.

"Can I help you?" the lady asks as they step outside.

"That's Rufus!" Adara cries.

The little boy looks at Adara, then at me. "Doggy!" he says, pointing at me. Rufus falls to the ground.

The lady sets the boy on the mat and grabs Rufus before Adara can. "This is your dog?" she asks.

Adara nods. "My grandma gave him to me before we moved."

The boy snatches Rufus from his mom. "My dog!" he says.

"Are you sure that's your dog, Adara?" Mom says. "Maybe he just looks like your dog."

"That's Rufus," Adara says. "I know it is."

Sniff...sniff... "She's right," I say. "It's Rufus!"

"You're Mrs. Keene, aren't you?" the lady says, walking over to Mom. The little boy toddles behind her, holding tight to Rufus as Adara scowls at him. "I'm Carrie Noble, and this is Theo. Theo's brother Jaden goes to your school."

"Oh, of course," Mom says. "Hello."

"Jaden forgot his lunch this morning," the lady explains. "So Theo and I walked it up to school. I'm not sure what happened. I saw Jaden on the playground, so I gave him his lunch. I talked to his teacher for a little bit, then Theo and I walked home. When we got here, I found this dog in the stroller with him. I have no idea where it came from."

"My dog!" the boy says again.

"Uh-oh," says Connor. "I don't think that little boy is going to give Rufus up."

Adara's eyes fill with water. "But Rufus is *my* dog, not his," she cries.

"Theo?" the lady says. "The dog belongs to this nice girl. We need to give it back to her."

Theo shakes his head hard. "My dog! Boy say *my* dog!"

"What boy?" Connor asks.

"Did a boy give you that dog?" Mrs. Noble asks Theo.

Theo nods.

"While I was talking to Mrs. Anderson?" Mrs. Noble asks.

Theo nods again.

Alex, I think. Alex must've given him to Theo. That's why he had Rufus's scent on him.

"Someone must have found Rufus on the playground while you were talking and thought he was Theo's dog," Mrs. Argus says.

"Who?" Connor asks.

"We'll probably never know," Mom says.

I know who! I know who! But it doesn't matter. What matters is that Adara gets her dog back.

"I'm so sorry," Mrs. Noble says to Adara. She tries to take Rufus from Theo, but he won't let her.

"My dog! My dog!" he cries.

"Maybe if you give the girl her dog, these people will let you pet their real dog," Mrs. Noble says.

Theo looks at me.

I sit and wag my tail.

I can tell Theo is thinking about petting me.

"Okay," Theo finally says. He hands Rufus to Adara, and then he throws his arms around me.

"Hi," I say, licking the top of his head. Mm. He's got applesauce in his hair. I LOVE applesauce. It's my favorite food!

"Hey, Theo. Do you want to do a trick with Buddy?" Connor asks.

Theo looks at Connor.

"Buddy can do lots of tricks," Connor says.

It's true. I can.

"Buddy, sit!" Connor says.

I sit.

"Buddy, shake!"

I lift my paw and Connor shakes it.

Theo smiles. Then, holding on to the railing, he toddles down the steps and runs to get a stick. "Fetch!" he says, throwing the stick.

Oh, I LOVE Fetch. It's my favorite game! I run to get the stick and bring it back to Theo.

Theo giggles.

"It's more fun to play with a real dog than a stuffed dog, isn't it, Theo?" Mrs. Noble asks.

"Yes!" Theo says.

"Yes!" I say.

"So Buddy was innocent all along," Connor says, scratching my ears.

"I guess he was," Mrs. Argus admits.

"Buddy, I'm sorry we ever doubted you," Mom says.

"I forgive you," I say.

Then Adara walks over to me. "Thanks, Buddy," she says, giving me a pat on the head. "Thanks for finding Rufus. You're a nice dog."

She likes me! Adara likes me!

"Ready to go home, Buddy?" Connor asks.

"Ready to go home," I say.

I've solved the case of the missing P-O-U-N-D Pet. Everyone knows I'm innocent. Everyone knows I'm a Good Dog!

I wonder if I'll get a reward when we get home. A liver treat would be a nice reward. I LOVE liver treats. They're my favorite food!

ABOUT THE AUTHOR

Dori Hillestad Butler is an award-winning author of more than 50 books for young readers, including The Haunted Library series and the King & Kayla series, which is the prequel to The Buddy Files. Her book *The Case of the Lost Boy* (The Buddy Files Book 1) won the 2011 Edgar Award for best juvenile mystery. Dori has been an active library volunteer, therapy-dog partner, and mentor to many young writers. She grew up in southern Minnesota, spent 19 years in Iowa, and now lives in the Seattle area. She loves visiting schools and libraries all over the country.

Made in the USA
Monee, IL
09 November 2020